# FOUR ENGLISH COMEDIES

Ben Jonson was born in 1572 at Westminster, the son of a minister, and educated at Westminster School. In about 1597 he worked for Henslowe, the theatre manager, and he led gatherings of writers at the Mermaid Tavern. His first major success was *Every Man in His Humour* (1598), but his finest plays were written after 1606: *Volpone* (1606), *Epicoene, or The Silent Woman* (1609), *The Alchemist* (1610) and *Bartholomew Fair* (1614). From 1616 he held a grant from James I and devised elaborate court masks, often with Inigo Jones. Jonson died in 1637.

William Congreve was born in 1670 in Yorkshire, spent his childhood in Ireland, where his father was on military service, and was a fellow-student to Swift at Kilkenny and Trinity College, Dublin. In 1691 he came to London to study law. He had already published verse and a novel when he achieved fame with his first comedy, *The Old Batchelor*, in 1693. His other plays included *The Double Dealer* (1694), *Love for Love* (1695) and *The Way of the World* (1700). Congreve, a friend of Steele and Pope and intimately attached to the Duchess of Marlborough, held various government sinecures. He died in 1729 and was buried in Westminster Abbey.

Oliver Goldsmith was born in 1730, the son of an Irish clergyman, and educated at Trinity College, Dublin, and in Edinburgh, where he studied medicine. In 1756 he returned destitute from wandering through Europe, and became a hackwriter of reviews and biographies. In 1761 he met Dr Johnson and became a member of 'The Club'. Among his works the best known are *The Vicar of Wakefield* (1766, written in 1762), *The Good-Natur'd Man* (1768), and *She Stoops to Conquer*, an immense success in 1773. Goldsmith died in 1774.

Richard Brinsley Sheridan was born in 1751, the son of an actor-elocutionist, and educated at Harrow. He escorted the singer Elizabeth Linley to France, fought two duels on her behalf, and married her in 1773. In 1775 he made a spectacular debut as a dramatist with three plays: *The Rivals*, *St Patrick's Day* and *The Duenna*, a comic opera. The following year he acquired Garrick's share in the Drury Lane Theatre which he managed until it was burnt down in 1809. *The School for Scandal* was produced in 1777 and *The Critic* in 1779. From 1780 until 1812 Sheridan was an M.P. and held government offices. In 1787–8 he made some celebrated speeches impeaching Warren Hastings. He died in 1816.